The Telltale Connection

3—

The Telltale Connection

Unsuspected Ties With the Frightening
World of Angels-Turned-Demons

George E. Vandeman

PACIFIC PRESS PUBLISHING ASSOCIATION
Boise, Idaho
Oshawa, Ontario, Canada

Cover illustration by Jim Pearson

Copyright © 1984 by
Pacific Press Publishing Association
Printed in United States of America
All Rights Reserved

Library of Congress Cataloging in Publication Data

Vandeman, George E.
  The telltale connection.

  1. Devil. 2. Demonology. 3. Occult sciences—Controversial literature. 3. Psychical research—Controversial literature. I. Title.
BT981.V36   1984   235'.4   84-22626

ISBN 0-8163-0581-1

Contents

The Telltale Connection

On the eighteenth of December, 1912, it was announced to the world that the remains of an early human fossil had been found in a shallow gravel pit near the village of Piltdown in the County of Sussex, England. Britain was proud, for the Piltdown Man was believed to be the earliest known human fossil.

But some forty years later another announcement was made. It had all been an out-and-out fake, the work of a person or persons unknown. Its lower jaw was not human at all, but that of a young female orangutan. Its teeth had been filed, and the hinge had been broken to prevent the discovery that it did not belong with the skull. British science was red-faced.

Charles Dawson, the discoverer, became the prime suspect. And though he had died thirty-seven years earlier, a monument to him was promptly removed. Through the years a number of others were suggested as possible suspects, but Dawson was still the front-runner.

But there was someone else who had haunted the Piltdown site during the excavation. He was a retired medical doctor who knew human anatomy well. He

was a chemist, much interested in both geology and
archaeology, and an avid collector of fossils. More than
that, he loved a good hoax. He loved adventure. He
was a writer gifted in manipulating the most complex
plots. And a motive was not hard to find, for he bore a
grudge against the British science establishment. Who
was he? None other than the creator of Sherlock
Holmes—Sir Arthur Conan Doyle!

So it was that John Hathaway Winslow, a writer of
our own time, found himself on the trail of the greatest
fictional detective of all time—Sherlock Holmes,
whose exploits became required reading for the police
forces of several nations. Winslow went public with his
astounding findings in the September issue of *Science
83*. And I think you'll agree that the case against Conan
Doyle, though circumstantial, is convincing to the
point of being overwhelming.

Doyle lived only seven or eight miles from the excavation site, and it appears that he visited it openly in
1912. Here was a doctor no longer in practice. At this
stage he was enjoying the rewards of a successful author. He was a prodigious walker, who often set forth
on long jaunts. There is little doubt that he often visited
the relatively unguarded site, or passed next to it and
peered over the hedge to observe progress. All he had
to do was watch out for the excavators.

The most difficult task was to concoct a convincing
creature, stain it to match the color of the Piltdown
gravel, and surround it with appropriate fossil remains
and implements. All this he was more than competent
to accomplish.

How could he have obtained the jawbone of an
orangutan? A former neighbor of his had recently returned from the Malay Peninsula, where his brother

was head of the Malay museums. And one of his museums had just purchased a large collection of animal specimens from Borneo. Orangutans live only in Borneo and Sumatra.

How would Doyle know how to file teeth to make them simulate human wear? Early in his medical practice he had moved into a house previously occupied by a dentist. Heaped about in great numbers were casts of human jaws.

How did he get just the right skull? He had a friend who had an immense collection of skulls and often sold them to those interested.

Some of the fossil mammal remains planted by the hoaxer were later identified as coming from the Mediterranean. How could Doyle have obtained them? He and his second wife had recently honeymooned on the Mediterranean and had visted the most likely sites. The timing of his travels was perfect.

On and on the clues fit together like pieces of a puzzle. But what about a motive? Why did he hold a grudge against the science establishment? Here, too, the evidence is convincing.

Arthur Conan Doyle was not only fascinated with science, but in his later years he had become a firm believer in Spiritualism. On the other hand, scientist Edwin Ray Lankester was a dedicated Darwinian evolutionist, probably evolution's staunchest defender. And he had no use for Spiritualists. He held them up to ridicule and was merciless in his attacks. He believed their claims were fraudulent, and he wanted desperately to catch them in the act.

For that purpose he attended a séance in the company of the American medium Henry Slade, who was the rage of British Spiritualists in the mid-1870s. There was to be communication with a spirit, and the spirit would write a message on a slate. But just after the slate was shown to those present, to demonstrate that it was clean, and before there was any noise of writing, Lankester grabbed the slate and discovered a message already on it. A magistrate agreed that fraud had taken place. And Henry Slade left England as quietly and quickly as possible.

Doyle was very unhappy about this exposure, and complained that it was not right to condemn all Spiritualists because of one instance of fraud. Doyle and Lankester were not friends!

Would it be surprising at all if Arthur Conan Doyle, master creator of fiction that he was, should find exquisite delight in bringing the same sort of embarrassment to British science that Lankester had brought to the Spiritualists? What more natural motive could there be?

Yes, *the telltale connection* that links Arthur Conan Doyle to Piltdown Man is very, very strong!

But there are other links, other ties, other connections that we must explore. Some interesting. And some very significant, linking even the two opposites, so often antagonistic to each other—evolution and spiritism. The one calling itself science; the other considered antiscientific.

In the days of Arthur Conan Doyle the theory of evolution had already done more than anything else to destroy faith in the Bible and in God Himself. But this left men and women adrift on a sea of chance—without a future, without hope. So where did they turn? By the thousands they turned to the psychic world, to the séance, to psychic phenomena—in an effort to replace what they had lost.

But there is a stronger tie between spiritism and evolution. For both reach back to the early morning of this planet. We find there the beginning of spiritism and its promises. And we find there the record of the first use of a psychic phenomenon to attract an audience.

True, we find no theory of evolution in the book of Genesis. But we do find, in the very first verse of the Bible, the clear statement that God is the Creator. It reads like this: "In the beginning God created the heaven and the earth." Genesis 1:1.

And it is that simple statement which evolution refuses to believe. Its challenge of God's creatorship and its substitution of a man-made theory of our beginnings in its place—here is the heart of evolutionary teaching.

Have you ever noticed that the quarrel of unbelievers with the Bible is usually concerned with the early chapters of Genesis? Evolution ties back to that Book as an open challenge of God's credibility.

In the case of spiritism, we find its beginning in the story of man's fall, recorded in the third chapter of the Bible. And there God is openly charged with not telling the truth.

Now I know that the story of man's fall is widely considered just a bit of folklore—amusing folklore at that. Give someone the clue, "She ate the apple." And you will get the response, "Eve." And the fact that there is no mention of an apple in the Genesis story is an indication of how little attention has been given to what happened there.

I ask you, *Could it be that Genesis 3 is not folklore at all, but rather the first boom of cosmic cannons in a continuing and escalating war that explains every strange thing that is happening today?*

Imagine, if you will, the impossible. Imagine that you were a cosmic reporter assigned to cover the creation of the planet Earth, to be an actual eyewitness to it all.

It was an exciting week. Accompanying the Creator and His entourage of angels as He moved down through the star-studded corridors of space—with galaxies and flashing suns on every side. And angel harps tuned their highest.

Then you reached a lonely spot near the edge of God's universe. You saw Him step out into the emptiness and speak words filled with all the power of the Infinite. The thunder of His voice resonated to distant worlds. And suddenly there it was, where a moment before there was nothing. A planet fresh from the Creator's hand, spinning in perfect orbit!

The whole week was spectacular beyond words. You've used all your best adjectives—and failed even to approach the reality. And then, on Friday afternoon, came God's masterpiece of creation, made in His own image—Adam and Eve!

You were glad when you were permitted to stay on, to cover further developments. But that prospect was not completely bright, for you knew that all was not well in God's universe. Heaven's highest and most privileged angel, one named Lucifer, had become dissatisfied over nothing. It seems that his own beauty convinced him that he ought to have the place of God. He was especially angry over the fact that the Son of God was to be the One to actually speak the planet Earth into existence. Why not Lucifer?

He had to be banished from heaven. There was no other way. But now he is here. And you remember how furious he was when he saw the exquisite beauty of the planet God had fitted up for Adam and Eve. You heard him cursing God and plotting to make this earth the headquarters of his rebellion.

The problem is that God has created Adam and Eve with the power to choose. He doesn't want any of His subjects to be robots. So this happy pair *could* rebel. It *could* happen. And that would be tragedy for the human race!

You heard God talking to Adam. And he said something like this: "Adam, I have given you the power to choose. You are not a robot. I will set before you life and death. And I expect you to be responsible for the choice you make. I hope you will choose life. But the decision is yours."

And God said to Adam, "I want to give you never-ending life. That is My plan. But I dare not give you immortality until I know you can be trusted with a life that never ends. In order to test your loyalty I have placed off bounds one tree in the Garden—just one tree. If you eat of its fruit you will be separating yourself from the Source of life, and you will die. That isn't a threat, Adam. Death is just the natural result of rebellion. I hope you will act responsibly. But you must choose. I cannot choose for you."

You were listening, too, the day God told the happy pair about Lucifer. He told them that He would not permit the fallen angel to follow them around the Garden. He could tempt them only if they approached the one forbidden tree. Adam and Eve talked it all over. And they couldn't imagine such a terrible thing as rebelling against the Creator they loved.

Then came that fateful day. Eve was walking alone as she approached that tree. Walking alone—and wondering aloud why God had placed that one tree off bounds. It didn't look dangerous. It was as beautiful as all the other trees. The serpent was sitting on one of its branches, contentedly eating the fruit. And the serpent began to talk to Eve. And she knew that serpents didn't have the power of speech, even in the Garden of Eden. She didn't know, though she should have known, that she was witnessing the first psychic phenomenon in this earth's history, that here was a daylight séance, with the serpent acting as a medium for the fallen angel.

You watched as the serpent invited the woman to eat, assuring her that it couldn't harm her. After all, wasn't he eating it himself?

You weren't the only one who wanted to cry out to warn her. Angels were watching. God was watching. But no one must interfere. You watched in breathless horror as she reached out, took the fruit, and ate. And then, when she felt no harm, she filled her arms with the beautiful fruit and took it to her husband.

You'll never forget the look of shock and terror in Adam's face when he saw what Eve had done. He knew that she must die. And he couldn't bear the thought of losing her. He didn't stop to think that God could create another companion for him—one as lovely as she. He just rashly, deliberately, knowing the consequences of his act, determined that if Eve must die, he would die with her. And the whole human race had, at that moment, entered the age of tears!

Well, you weren't there. And I wasn't there. There was no press coverage. There were no television cameras. No press conferences. It wasn't that the press was barred. There wasn't any press!

Let's read it—just as the Bible tells it. First, this is what God told Adam. This is the warning, given in the deepest love and concern: "The Lord God commanded the man, saying, Of every tree of the garden thou mayest freely eat: But of the tree of the knowledge of good and evil, thou shalt not eat of it: for in the day that thou eatest thereof thou shalt surely die." Genesis 2:16, 17.

Was this a threat? No. Is it a threat if I tell you that if you jump from the top of the Empire State Building you will die? Of course not. God was only telling Adam what the consequence of a wrong choice would be.

But the serpent openly contradicts what God has said. Listen: "The serpent said unto the woman, Ye shall not surely die: For God doth know that in the day ye eat thereof, then your eyes shall be opened, and ye shall be as gods, knowing good and evil." Genesis 3:4, 5.

The battle is out in the open. The fallen angel has charged God with being untruthful, with withholding the highest good from His subjects. He's still making the same charge today. And millions are believing it!

Think about *this* for a moment. If the fall of man was not planned or programmed by the Creator, it follows that *it didn't have to happen*. Let us suppose, then, that Adam's wife, rather than entering into conversation with the serpent, had turned pale at the sight and sound of a serpent talking, and had set the world's first track record in her flight back to the safety of her husband's company.

If only the story of Genesis 3 could be rewritten!

Or what about *this*? God is all-powerful. Nothing is too hard for Him. That conversation between Eve and the serpent took only a few short moments. Adam's decision took only seconds. Time is under the control of its Creator. Why couldn't He just lift that short segment of time out of history and close it up as if it had never happened? Should the destiny of the human race depend upon the decisions of a single hour?

But no! A God of love and integrity would never stoop to such manipulation of events. He will never deceive His subjects about what has gone before. The tragic story of man's fall cannot be deleted. It cannot be rewritten. It happened just as the book of Genesis tells it. The woman saw a serpent talking. She listened. She believed. And *belief was the enemy!*

Do you realize what a strong link there is between deception and death? Seldom does one deceive another for any good purpose. Certainly not the fallen angel. He deceives men and women with only one thing in mind—to utterly destroy them. When he peddles his deceptions, he is peddling death—death from which there is no recovery, no resurrection. And you'll be amazed to see the variety and the attractiveness of the packaging he uses!

Yet in spite of the endless variation, the constant changing of labels, and the ever more alluring giftwrap, the strategy of the fallen angel and his invisible army of angels-turned-demons is still the same today as it was in the Garden of Eden. His use of disguise. His use of a medium. His use of psychic phenomena to capture a mind and throw it off guard. His challenge of God's integrity. His suggestion that God is withholding that which is good. His promise that you will never die, no matter how you live. His promise that rebellion will lead to a state like that of the gods. These are the earmarks of the great deceiver's philosophy.

Remember his words, "Ye shall not surely die." And "ye shall be as gods." Watch for them. For no matter where you find them, and no matter how cleverly they are rephrased, they shout one warning, "Lucifer was here!"

Yes, you will be shocked to your toes as you see what is going on in the unseen world!

This generation, unfortunately, is an easy mark for anything sensational, anything supernatural, any package that comes complete with miracles. Ours is a generation that loves magic. It is fascinated by the unknown, by the invisible, by auras and pyramid power and biorhythms and whatever is new.

Millions are saying, "Entertain us. Excite us. Show us magic. Dazzle our eyes with the supernatural. Boggle our minds. Mystify us. Cast a spell over us. Overwhelm our senses. Sweep us off our feet. Promise us fun and fame and heaven too. And we'll follow you anywhere!"

The generation honored with the personal presence of Jesus was not unlike our own. Constantly it was demanding, "Show us a sign that You are who You claim to be. Light up the sky at midnight. Leap off the pinnacle of the temple. Strike the hated Romans dead. Give us a sign!"

But Jesus never confused magic with power. He came not to manipulate minds, but to transform them at the sinner's request. He came not to take the throne, but to be crucified. Not to be a King, but a Sacrifice. He said to those who demanded to know His identity, "When you have lifted up the Son of Man, then you will know who I am." John 8:28, NIV.

"When you have lifted Me up. When you have crucified Me. When you have scorned Me and mocked Me and laughed at Me. When you have driven spikes into My hands. When you have hung Me between heaven and earth on a despised Roman cross and dared Me to come down if I could. When you have left Me to die without even a drink of cold water. *Then* you will know who I am!"

And yes, when He hung there on that splintery cross, they knew. The thief on the cross beside Him knew who He was. The Roman centurion knew. And the enemies of Jesus knew. The haughty Caiaphas. And Pilate. And many a man left that cross with tortured conscience and unclean hands because he had joined with the mob in crucifying the very Son of God!

That generation, and ours, had been given a sign—the sign of the Son of God dying in man's place. There is no greater sign!

You and I will have to decide whether we want a magician or a Saviour. And there's no better time than now to make our choice!

Playing Games With Death

The legend says that it happened in the streets of Baghdad.

A merchant sent his servant to the market. But soon he returned, trembling and greatly agitated, and said to his master, "Down in the marketplace I was jostled by a woman in the crowd, and when I turned around I saw it was Death that jostled me. She looked at me and made a threatening gesture. Master, please lend me your horse, for I must hasten away to avoid her. I will ride to Samarra and there I will hide, and Death will not find me."

The merchant lent him his horse, and the servant galloped away in a cloud of dust.

A little later the merchant himself went to the marketplace and saw Death standing in the crowd. He said to her, "Why did you frighten my servant this morning? Why did you make a threatening gesture?"

"That was not a threatening gesture," said Death. "It was only a start of surprise. I was astonished to see him in Baghdad, for *I have an appointment with him tonight in Samarra!*"

Only a legend—out of the streets of Baghdad. But it

paints a graphic picture of the fatalism that is gripping countless minds today. For millions of frustrated individuals have decided that this weary planet, with every man on it, has an appointment with the death angel—its wings bathed in atomic power and propelling us swiftly to oblivion.

We try to forget. We spend long hours in the pursuit of pleasure and profit. We fall in love with toyland. We protest what is happening. We rebel against a future that we cannot control. But sooner or later, even in the busy marketplace, man is jostled by the death angel, rudely reminded of her presence. And what else can he do but begin a wild ride to Samarra, hoping to find someplace to hide, some barrier behind which death shall forget to look?

Death is on the way out. Because of what Jesus did on Calvary, death will one day be destroyed. But in the meantime, death is still on the loose. And this planet is the cemetery of the universe—the place where everybody dies!

A little child in Northern Ireland saw his father gunned down at his own front door. Night after night, following that tragedy, little David would scream as he relived that terrible moment in his dreams. Night after night he would kneel by his bed and say, "Please, God, can't Daddy come down from heaven just for a minute so I can see him? I won't keep him. I'll let him go back."

Why didn't God answer that little boy's prayer? Is there a reason? Doesn't God care?

Yes, of course He cares! And yes, I believe there is a reason.

· I believe, too, that the cruel enemy of us all, who loves nothing better than to deceive and destroy, would gladly take advantage of little David's tears and *appear* to answer his prayer. Hundreds of times, in a cloak of false compassion, the fallen angel has *seemingly* brought back a loved one, just for a minute, so he could be seen and even touched.

But what if it is all a cruel hoax? What if that heartless enemy of ours is taking lying advantage of our loneliness and our tears, using our grief to entrap us?

To believe in the Lord Jesus is a wonderful thing—a saving thing. But if we believe in a hoax, *belief is the enemy!*

I think of the experience of a woman in Scotland. During the war she had received word that her husband was missing in action. Many months passed, and it seemed that surely he was dead. Friends urged her to try to contact him through a séance, and she felt that she might find there a measure of comfort.

Again and again she made contact with a spirit she believed to be that of her husband. The voice, she was sure, was that of her loved one. The apparition looked like her loved one. Repeatedly they talked over many things.

Then one day, months later, her husband walked unannounced through the front door, alive and well. He had never been dead, or even wounded!

Is it any wonder that the woman became bitter toward all religion? What a heartless hoax!

There is lying and fraud and trickery in the psychic world. But there is no mistake more dangerous than to believe that it is *all* fraud and trickery. Jesus warned us concerning our day, "For false Christs and false prophets will appear and perform great signs and miracles to deceive even the elect—if that were possible." Matthew 24:24, NIV.

No one is in greater danger than the man who thinks spiritism is all magic and trickery and fraud, just waiting to be exposed by someone as discerning as himself. Because someday something will happen to *him*—something that can't be explained away. And he'll tumble right into the trap!

Ever since it first coldly introduced itself on this planet, death has been a mystery. Everybody dies. So it is only natural that we should want to know what happens on the other side of this final experience. But in our day the popular interest in death is approaching an obsession. There are classes in death and dying, manuals on how to die. Mothers rock their dead babies, and fathers hammer in the coffin nails. Dying is treated as an adventure, a romance.

But I am uncomfortable about all this cozying up with death. What if it becomes not only an obsesison but an involvement, a cozying up with the fallen angel who is the author of death?

This generation, like those before it, continues to play its dangerous games with death. But in our day something new has been added. For now we are bombarded with the stories of those who say they have personally experienced death and have come back to tell us about it.

You've heard the reports—all strangely similar. Leaving their bodies. Long, dark tunnels. Then grassy slopes. And a being of light. And they don't want to come back to their bodies. Most significant of all, these people aren't afraid of death anymore. And they don't believe the Bible anymore. They think they have found a better source of information.

Were these people really dead? Or just *near* death? Evidently they were not irreversibly dead, for all were resuscitated. Evidently these experiences are just the malfunctioning of a mind almost gone. There are many similar out-of-body experiences in drug literature.

But if these stories represent simply the misfiring of a mind near death how is it that hundreds of minds are misfiring in almost the same way? Something is going on here. Something strange. Is it possible that some external power, some intelligent and highly motivated entity, may be stepping in to control these weakened and malfunctioning minds? If so, who would be suspect? Who could be so motivated?

Some say these experiences prove that there is life after death. But do they—if those involved didn't really die? And some say these reports prove that the Bible is true. But how can they be supportive of the Bible when they are in strong disagreement with it?

How are they in disagreement? In what they say about what happens at death. Listen to this clear scripture: "The living know that they shall die: but the dead know not any thing." Ecclesiastes 9:5.

The verse that follows is also interesting, for it says: "Also their love, and their hatred, and their envy, is now perished." Ecclesiastes 9:6.

There is an equally strong statement in the Psalms. "Put not your trust in princes, nor in the son of man, in whom there is no help. His breath goeth forth, he returneth to his earth; in that very day his thoughts perish." Psalm 146:3, 4.

According to the Bible, the dead know nothing. Their thoughts have perished. Certainly there can be no communication with those who don't know anything and can't think. The Bible has the dead quietly sleeping in their graves till the day of the resurrection when Jesus calls them to life. They know nothing of what is happening to loved ones who still live. According to the Bible we do not go to our reward at death, one at a time. Rather, our Lord has planned that we all go together when He returns. The resurrection is the hope of the Christian. Listen to the words of the apostle Paul as he describes it: "The Lord himself shall descend from heaven with a shout, with the voice of the archangel, and with the trump of God: and the dead in Christ shall rise first: Then we which are alive and remain shall be caught up together with them in the clouds, to meet the Lord in the air: and so shall we ever be with the Lord." 1 Thessalonians 4:16, 17.

What a day of reunion! Friends and loved ones long separated by death—now together again, nevermore to part. Little children carried from their graves by angels and placed in their mothers' arms. What a day! Would you want it any other way? Would you want to settle for some grassy slope?

Did you notice that, according to these recent reports, everybody goes to the same reward, the same grassy slope—regardless of how they have lived? It is that way in all of spiritism. Good and bad alike all go to the same place. There is no judgment to determine what a man's reward should be.

And did you notice that no one sees God or Jesus on those grassy slopes? But there is a being of light. And it is reported that that being of light even laughs at their sins. Would Jesus ever laugh at sin—when it was our sins that crushed out His life?

Can you guess who that being of light might be? Listen to this: "And no marvel; for Satan himself is transformed into an angel of light." 2 Corinthians 11:14.

Do you see whose philosophy it is that runs like a thread through all of this? Do you see *the telltale con-*

nection? Do you see how it all ties back to the words of the serpent in the Garden of Eden? "You will not surely die." That's what the fallen angel said then. He's still saying it in a thousand ways. Only now he's calling it science. And thousands who would never go near a *séance* are swept into the net!

These experiences haven't proved a thing—except that Satan, just as the Bible says, is furious because he knows that his time is short. Spiritism is sweeping the world. And only those who know the Bible, and hold onto it for dear life, will escape!

"You will not surely die." The whole house of spiritism would collapse overnight if that false concept were not so readily accepted by fallen humanity. But voices everywhere are echoing those words. And millions are believing the lie!

It's only one more step to the epidemic of seeking altered states of consciousness that is rampant today. And along with this, fitting like a glove, is the idea of a universal energy that flows through man, making him the possessor of divine power, making him a part of God. Remember? "You will be as gods."

And if man, simply by connecting himself with this psychic force, tapping this universal energy, can make himself a god, what need has he of a Saviour? What need has he of repentance? Guilt can be forgotten—now that the power of God is within himself!

Do you see how dangerous these ideas are—and how fatal?

But that is just what Satan wants. He knows that he himself is doomed. And he has determined to take the whole human race with him to destruction—if he can!

That's why he is telling this generation that death is not so bad after all, that it is nothing to fear, that no one ever really dies. That's why he tells everyone who will listen that there is no judgment, that good and bad all go to the same place, regardless of how they have lived. He is bribing men and women with a false hope that God calls a "refuge of lies."

But that refuge of lies will be swept away. No man can escape death by cozying up to it and calling it a friend!

Listen! Are you satisfied to look forward to nothing but a little bit of grass, approached by a long, dark tunnel? Are you interested at all in a future that has no place for God and Jesus? What sort of paradise would it be if all the mass murderers and rapists and madmen were there to terrorize eternity?

Wouldn't you rather have the heaven that Jesus has prepared for you—where sin and death and heartache and tears are forever shut out? A place that is lighted by the glory that streams from the throne of God. A place where there is no night. A city with gates and streets and fabulous homes that are real—with your name over the door of one of them. Where you can see Jesus face to face. Where yours can be the companionship of angels. And friends and loved ones will never part again!

And there's so much more! Flowers that never fade. Leaves that never fall. Beauty beyond description. Space travel to other worlds. Endless opportunities to explore and understand God's vast creation. Nothing will be left out that could possibly contribute to your happiness!

This is the heaven that Lucifer lost. This is the home that will never be his again. That's why he's determined that you shall never experience it. He's going to belittle it—play it down—ridicule it—counterfeit it—lie about it. And he'll smile in hellish glee if you decide it's nothing you want! But the choice is yours. You don't have to miss out!

Today the way seems long and weary. It may seem that the long night of tears and trouble will never be finished. But it will, friend. It will. Swiftly, so swiftly, it will change. Think what it will be to breathe the freshness of the morning and know that it will never end. Suddenly it's heaven! Suddenly it's home!

Think about that home. Think about it often. Let it fill your mind. Let it give you something to live for. Let it take your loneliness away. The Saviour wants you to have it. Even now He is out on the road calling your name. Calling you to Himself. Why not take His hand just now— and let Him lead you home?

Psychic Counterfeits

Dark clouds scowled over Lhasa, the mysterious forbidden city of Tibet. The year was 1855. And the Dalai Lama was dead!

It was believed that a Mongolian hermit had slipped poison into the ruler's butter tea. But the hermit had escaped. And *someone* must be punished!

Late that night, in the temple room of the Potala—the thousand-room palace of the Dalai Lama—a séance was called. The Oracle, the state prophet of Tibet, would invoke the gods to learn who had killed their supreme lama.

Tempu Gergan, the wealthy and respected minister of finance, stood nervously at the edge of the group. He had been warned that afternoon that he might be named the culprit. And he knew it was not unlikely, for only recently he had accused the Oracle of being unreliable. Would he pass by an opportunity for revenge?

All was now ready. The Oracle sat on his throne, wearing the ceremonial robes. On his head was a massive helmet of silver and gold, embellished with five human skulls.

A high lama wafted incense into the seer's face. Behind him a choir of priests chanted weirdly. Facing the Oracle, a living Buddha in a spine-chilling chant was calling upon the three-headed, six-armed demon-god to take possession of the seer.

"Come hither, mighty Pehar. Tell us who killed the Dalai Lama."

Tempu's breath was choking him. He wanted to scream. But a hypnotic spell kept his eyes on the Oracle.

The face of the Oracle had undergone a terrifying change. It was no longer the face of a priest, but the leering face of Pehar. The Oracle was now fully demon-possessed!

Tempu stood cold but perspiring. The ground seemed to sway beneath him as he watched from behind a pillar.

"I see a golden cup with a demon dancing upon the brim," muttered the Oracle. "There is a strange priest offering the cup to the Dalai Lama. He wears a high-peaked hat and tattered garments."

He was describing the Mongolian. But the demon voice went on, "I see around the holy one bags of gold and silver. A hand offers the silver to the strange priest. The face—I cannot see the face. Yes, it is coming—"

Tempu knew instinctively that he would be named. He flung himself out the door and down the passageway. Pausing only a moment in a small room, he discarded his rich brocades and strode on as a peasant pilgrim. But already he could hear a crescendo of voices, "Tempu Gergan is the man! Seize him!"

He wanted to dash madly away. But he must look like a poor pilgrim. Would the eternal stairs never end?

Finally he was clear of the building and headed for

the city wall. He heard a shout behind him, "Block the stairs! No one must leave the palace!"

He had escaped just in time. Silently he slipped over the wall where a trusted servant waited with two horses.

He had escaped. But he would never see his beloved city of Lhasa again. An innocent man would spend the rest of his days in exile—all because of an unreliable priest, aided by lying demons!

You say, "I would never attend a séance or have anything to do with demons. So I'm safe."

But don't be too sure!

The winds are blowing out of the East with gale force. Western fascination with Eastern mysticism can no longer be considered a passing fad. True, the traditions of Eastern worship are filtered through Western secularism to make them appear less threatening. But they are here—and here to stay. Basic occult philosophy—fresh-labeled and unrecognized—is pervading our society. Transcendental meditation has been taught in our schools—as science. It has become popular to talk of past lives—and karma. And, believe it or not, it is said that firewalking—yes, walking across hot coals with bare feet—could be called almost a trend in southern California.

But call it what you will, Eastern worship is built upon a concept completely foreign to the gospel of Jesus Christ. Eastern religion, like nearly all false religion, is a gospel of salvation by works. It is man saving himself.

Call it what you will, Eastern meditation is not science. It is a religion. Regardless of claims to the contrary, it is Vedantic Hinduism. Its initiation rite is a religious ceremony. Its mantras are related to Hindu deities. And its goal is to attain the state of Hindu God-realization, to recognize our true self as divine.

Call it what you will, reincarnation, with its karma, is a cruel counterfeit of the cross of Calvary. It is man saying to God, "I don't need a Saviour. I'll pay for my own sins—even if it takes a thousand lives to do it!"

Don't you hear in it all the echo of the serpent's words, "Ye shall not surely die" and "Ye shall be as gods"? The telltale connection is too plain to miss!

And call it what you will, Eastern mysticism is riddled with demons. Listen to this: "They made Him jealous with strange gods; With abominations they provoked Him to anger. They sacrificed to demons who were not God, To gods whom they have not known, New gods who came lately, Whom your fathers did not dread." Deuteronomy 32:16, 17, NASB.

Have you ever wondered how it is that people, century after century, can bow down to gods of wood or stone—gods that cannot think—hideous gods that no worshiper could love—gods that they would escape if only they could? Have you blamed it to the backwardness of the East?

No, it isn't all backwardness. The power of those Eastern gods is not in the wood or in the stone. It is not in the idols themselves. It isn't their hideousness alone that inspires fear. It's the demons that inhabit them. Listen to what the apostle Paul says: "What do I mean then? That a thing sacrificed to idols is anything, or that an idol is anything? No; but I say that the things which the Gentiles sacrifice, they sacrifice to demons, and not to God; and I do not want you to become sharers in demons." 1 Corinthians 10:19, 20, NASB.

Can we reach into the Eastern fire and not be

burned? Can we take to ourselves what looks harm-less—and close our eyes to the Satanism, the human sacrifice, the demon possession, and all the rest?

There seems to be a death wish at work in Eastern mysticism. There are demon gods that stand at the gate of death and beckon the worshipers through. Like the serpent in Eden, they make death the door to the future—and the door to becoming a god. What a cruel hoax!

But has the fallen angel exhausted all his resources in the East? No. Never. He isn't limited to a little black bag or a tool box. He has a whole supermarket of sub-tle, unrecognized, mislabeled, gift-wrapped offerings just waiting for unsuspecting customers who think they are safe because they've never attended a séance!

Yes, you have to be wide awake and on your toes to keep from bumping into some slender thread of the web he is building around this whole planet!

Ever since the fallen angel began stalking the human race in the Garden of Eden he has been engaged in a desperate race for the minds of men. And he hasn't left a single avenue to the mind unexplored or unexploited!

Rock and roll. Harmless, you say. Just too loud. That's why you ask your teenagers to shut the door. But Bob Larson, former rock-and-roll performer and composer and now national radio commentator, has a different opinion. He says, "Rock and roll is the agency which Satan is using to possess this generation *en masse*. I have seen with my own eyes teenagers who have become demon-possessed while dancing to rock and roll music."

He points out that "there is no difference between the repetitive movements of witch doctors and tribal dancers and the dances of American teenagers." Both have the same hypnotic beat and the same potential for demon possession.

And listen to this—also from Bob Larson, author of *Rock and Roll, the Devil's Diversion*. Read especially pages 133-136.

"One of the most uncanny stories I have ever heard was related to me by a close friend of mine. For several weeks he dealt with a sixteen-year-old boy who by his own admission communed with demon spirits. One day [the boy] asked my friend to turn on the radio to a rock and roll station. As they listened, this teenager would relate, just prior to the time the singer on the recording would sing them, the words to songs he had never heard before. When asked how he could do this the sixteen-year-old replied that the same demon spirits that he was acquainted with had inspired the songs. Also he explained that while on acid trips he could hear demons sing some of the very songs he would later hear recorded by psychedelic rock groups."

What do you think of that?

Yes, the fallen angel is peddling his wares everywhere—under a thousand false labels. And if they were all exposed for what they really are, he would have a thousand more. But keep in mind that he would not be so successful if he were not offering what this generation wants!

For instance, this generation doesn't want the responsibility that goes with belief in a Creator. It prefers to trace its origin to some ancient sea or to some cosmic accident. Or to Von Daniken's astronauts. Von Daniken, the author of three well-known books, may not know how to reason logically or consistently, but he knows how to jimmy the facts to fit his changing and contradictory theories. And he knows how to sell books!

The truth is that today's liberal society is open to *any* alternate to the Genesis account of creation.

And millions today prefer to get their guidance from the stars rather than order their lives by the only safe guide—the Word of God. This in spite of the complete unreliability of the horoscopes they follow.

A French statistician by the name of Michel Gauquelin has been putting astrology to the test for more than twenty years, reports the June issue of *Science 84*. On one occasion he put out a newspaper ad offering free personalized horoscopes. A hundred and fifty people responded. To each of them he sent the same identical horoscope and asked how well it fit. Ninety-four percent said they recognized themselves.

It was the horoscope of mass murderer Dr. Marcel Petiot!

Well, doesn't our Lord have something better for us than that? I believe He does. This is what He says: "I will instruct thee and teach thee in the way which thou shalt go: I will guide thee with mine eye." Psalm 32:8, KJV.

What could be better than that? To have our Lord personally guide us. Not the stars, but He who made the stars!

But now listen to what He says through the prophet Isaiah. We'll read it from the Today's English Version:

"Let your astrologers come forward and save you—
  those people who study the stars,
  who map out the zones of the heavens
  and tell you from month to month
  what is going to happen to you.
They will be like bits of straw,
  and a fire will burn them up!

They will not even be able to save themselves—"

Our Lord doesn't want us to be deceived. He doesn't want us to be conned by the enemy. He doesn't want us to get off the track and lose out in the end. That's why He expressly forbids His people to have anything to do with the occult—not just the astrologers, but the whole occult system. Listen to this: "There shall not be found among you any one that maketh his son or his daughter to pass through the fire, or that useth divination [fortune-teller], or an observer of times [astrologer], or an enchanter [magician], or a witch, or a charmer [hypnotist], or a consulter with familiar spirits [medium possessed with a spirit or a "guide"], or a wizard [clairvoyant or psychic], or a necromancer [medium who consults the dead]. For all that do these things are an abomination unto the Lord." Deuteronomy 18:10-12.

And I think you know what abomination means! Evidently our Lord just isn't on very good terms with the occult. He just doesn't want His people to be deceived and drawn into the devil's net!

Yet the very things God has forbidden are increasing in popularity every day! Yes, we have an enemy who is determined to destroy everyone he can. He would destroy the whole human race right now if God would permit it. He delights in violence and war. He loves to see masses of people swept into sudden death without a chance to repent.

To bring about this destruction he will use every disguise he can, every deception he can, every lie he can. He is delighted when men and women think he doesn't exist, or when they think of him as a horrible monster with hoofs and horns. Such ideas leave them completely unprepared for meeting him as an angel of light.

The fallen angel's hatred of God, and especially of

Jesus, knows no bounds. He is determined to counterfeit everything that is true and right and good. You have seen how he has counterfeited the future life, how he has distorted the facts about death. You have seen how he takes advantage of loneliness and tears and offers the false comfort of cummunication with the dead.

Satan is the great impersonator. And he has millions of helpers, invisible to us, who are almost as clever as he in impersonation. Remember that they are all fallen angels, with the intelligence of angels and with supernatural power. And they have had thousands of years of experience in their work of deception. They watch us, know all about us, and then trap us—too many of us. They impersonate dead people—and living people. They pose as residents of other worlds. They will yet try to counterfeit the second coming of our Lord. And Satan himself will impersonate Jesus. And almost everybody will bow down!

Do you begin to see what is going on in the invisible world? Our only safety is in letting the Lord Jesus lead us through this treacherous end time that is so mined with deception!

> Beneath the cross of Jesus
>   I fain would take my stand,
> The shadow of a mighty rock
>   Within a weary land;
> A home within the wilderness.
>   A rest upon the way,
> From the burning of the noontide heat,
>   And the burden of the day.

The Truth About Psychic Healing

I have here two newspaper articles. This one, dated January 11, 1978, and clipped from the *San Francisco Chronicle*, is titled "Skeptics of Mind Power Call It Superstition." And it says:

"If you suspect that UFOs may be real. . . .If you think the Bermuda Triangle is a dangerous place. . . . If you lend even half an ear to any of these beliefs—and there seem to be millions of Americans who do—well, man, there are some scientists and scholars who are mighty worried about you.

"They think you are being gulled, and they see the rise of cult and occult as a sickness of our times. For them the issue is science versus superstition."

But only a little more than six years later, on April 3, 1984, the *Oakland Tribune*, just across the Bay from San Francisco, carried an extensive article entitled "Psychics get foothold in the sciences." It carries over onto much of page two and is followed the next day by a second part. It is favorable in tone and could be summed up in these few words: "If psi works, why not use it?"

Are we about to witness a wedding of psi and science? It just could be. Did you know that John F. Kennedy University in Orinda, just beyond the Oakland hills, actually has an accredited parapsychology department?

Parapsychology has wanted all along to be known as a science, and for that reason has kept very quiet about its ties with the occult. Yet its strongest evidence comes from mediums, and without mediums it would collapse.

Parapsychology is the study of occult phenomena. And you can't go very far in the study of occult phenomena without encountering psychic healing in some form. Most every spirit medium has some ability to heal. You see, then, that the various forms of psychic healing are actually a subdivision of parapsychology.

Now science and psi, science and the occult, Western medicine and psychic healing, have wanted nothing to do with each other. But things are changing, in spite of the fact that parapsychology still calls itself a science. More and more physicians are endorsing psychic, or mediumistic, healing. And the door is being opened slightly even to witchcraft.

Physicians make up a large part of the 1500-member Academy of Parapsychology and Medicine, which gives much of its attention to research and psychic healing. Its president, Dr. Robert A. Bradley, is a medium. He is the inventor of the Bradley method of natural childbirth, which he says is an idea he received from one of his spirit guides. The primary purpose of the academy is to integrate science and medicine with the occult.

In Great Britain, the World Federation of Healers, with nine thousand members, has been given government permission to treat patients in fifteen hundred hospitals in that country. And this same federation, made up largely of professed mediums, has been given membership in the United Nations Association.

Former astronaut Edgar Mitchell, a parapsychology enthusiast, is said to be working hard to integrate psychic healing with traditional medicine. He believes that "psychic healers can become valuable adjuncts to hospital staffs, to general practitioners and to clinics." Yet there is something strange about his enthusiasm, for he also says that the power of psychic methodology "can be as dangerous as atomic energy; in reality I think it is even more so."

Strange, isn't it, to be so enthusiastic about something that dangerous?

Some qualified medical doctors are actually referring patients to mediums and occultists these days—to men like Dr. Robert Leichtman, for instance, who is a physician, psychic, and psychic researcher. He diagnoses from the spirit world. But word of his abilities has spread fast among his fellow MDs, and he diagnoses several hundred cases a year for them, with accuracy above the 90 percent level.

Dr. Elisabeth Kübler-Ross, the famous authority on death and dying, is deeply involved in the the occult, along with her partner and friend Dr. Raymond Moody, author of the best-seller *Life After Life*. It is said that Kübler-Ross has five spirit guides. "Salem" is her favorite.

Yes, things are changing. Science and psi are putting away their differences. And hypnosis is now everyday stuff.

"But wait!" you say. "What's wrong with hypnosis? It doesn't have any connection with the occult, does it?"

Well, you decide.

You've heard of mesmerism and its animal magnetism, popular in the last century. The mesmeric trance and the spiritistic trance were one and the same. And every occult phenomena found in mesmerism is found in modern hypnosis. Both are spiritistic, though Anton Mesmer, like the parapsychologists of today, preferred to identify with science. In essence, modern hypnotism *is* mesmerism.

In Satan's race for the minds of men, for the control of the will and the conscience, it is only natural that hypnotism should be one of his favorite tools. For he knows that hypnosis is a direct avenue to the mind. And he knows that when the mind is surrendered to another, even for some seemingly good purpose, he or one of his helpers can step in and take control. The gate is open.

Never forget that the conscience operates through the mind. When the mind is abdicated, so is the conscience. And never forget the fact that the mind once breached, the lock once pried, is never so strong again!

And the trouble is that reading labels doesn't help much. For hypnosis may even be slipped in under so harmless-sounding a label as "scientific relaxation."

Ever hear of Silva Mind Control? Or the now defunct Mind Dynamics? Classes like these promise you almost everything.

And testimonials are glowing. One girl insisted, "Besides finding that you can have anything you want, that you are the reason for everything, you also find that you can't be sad or depressed anymore." Is it any wonder that people sign up?

But Dr. Elmer Green, an outspoken critic who has even debated one of the groups on television, points out that most of these companies use nothing more than variations of hypnosis. He says that students in these organizations "go through a four-day program of intense hypnotic education in order to do the things they demonstrate."

Do you see now why Solomon, the wise man, gives us this counsel? "Keep thy heart [your mind] with all diligence; for out of it are the issues of life." Proverbs 4:23.

Well, what about yoga? You say, "I do yoga exercises. But that's just a way to relax the body and the mind. It's not Hinduism at all. And no demons are involved. So it's perfectly safe."

Are you sure?

The goal of yoga, says researcher John Weldon, is "for the yoga devotee to realize that he is one with Brahman, the highest impersonal Hindu God." And the physical exercises are designed to prepare one to receive this idea into his mind and body. Yoga is pure occultism. And meditation is the operative principle of yoga.

There are tremendous risks in the practice of yoga, especially Kundalini yoga. For a single mistake can mean insanity or sudden death. And demonic power is never far away.

Jesus spent a great deal of His time in healing. He spent more time in healing than in preaching. His compassion for human suffering knew no bounds. He didn't want anyone to hurt.

Wouldn't you expect, then, that the enemy—the fallen angel who is out to destroy all he can—wouldn't you expect him to give a high priority to counterfeit healing? And believe me, he hasn't missed the chance!

Psychic healing is becoming more popular every day.

Nobody wants to die. And when life is threatened, men and women will go anywhere, and pay any price, for even a promise of being well again.

There are psychic diagnosticians who follow in the steps of Edgar Cayce, who first developed his diagnosis from hypnosis.

Some healers achieve an accuracy approaching that of Cayce. Some of them never see the patient. Some of them use a device, such as a rod or pendulum, in their diagnosing. But the power is not in the device. It is in the operator. And the degree of success is proportionate to the degree of the healer's involvement with the spirit world, with the occult. Most of them know that spirits do the healing. But not all wish to identify themselves with the demonic. They may say the healing comes from their own "higher self."

Did you know that Cayce came to be much concerned about the nature of the power that operated through him? The time came when he suspected that "the devil might be tempting me to do his work by operating through me when I was conceited enough to think God had given me special power."

But Cayce, like so many others, was trapped. He was unable to outsmart or to stop the forces that worked through him.

There is something very interesting about psychic prescriptions. Some of them are just simple, harmless, old-fashioned ideas. And some of them are for the latest drugs—even though the healer may have no medical training whatever and may not even be able to read. He may be simply repeating what a voice in his ear is telling him.

And think about this: Some of these psychic prescriptions may not work at all if used by a physician with no occult ties. And some of them may be dangerous if used by a non-psychic physician, but perfectly harmless if used by an occult healer. In one instance a potent drug was prescribed in a quantity that would kill a dozen people. But evidently the healer's patient was unharmed!

Keep in mind that often a psychic diagnosis is wrong. Time is lost and real harm done. And even when apparent healing does take place, it is usually temporary. Often the illness is simply transferred to another part of the body—or worse, to the mind!

But whatever may be said to the contrary, there are cures. The supernatural is at work. And there are some undeniable miracles of healing. If you are ill—even terminally ill—there are places where you can go and be healed. But are you willing to pay the price? And do you know what the price is?

A patient appeared at the door of a healer who had been making some striking claims in newspaper ads. She told the healer that the doctors had diagnosed her as having a serious blood disease, possibly leukemia.

The healer replied, "I'm not a medical doctor. I treat with the mind and use hypnosis. The medical profession doesn't have a cure for leukemia. But we have cured leukemia. We have cured cancer, even terminal cancer." Then she outlined the procedure that she would use.

"Lend me your mind," she said, "to remove the debris and get your mind functioning properly." The mind would then purify the blood, and the body would then function as it should.

The patient turned out to be a policewoman who had secretly recorded the conversation. The healer was later arrested.

Notice. "Lend me your mind." I say again, There are places where you can go and be healed. But the price of healing is the surrender of your mind. Are you willing to pay such a staggering price? Are you willing to sell yourself into lifetime slavery to the spirit world, to the enemy of the Lord Jesus?

Some, of course, even with their eyes wide open, are willing to make such a fearful bargain. Listen to this from the psychic surgeon Edivaldo: "If the devil can relieve pain, open up a stomach and remove an ulcer, then I prefer the devil!"

We come now to psychic surgery. I confess that not many weeks ago I believed that all psychic surgery was outright fraud, accomplished by sleight of hand. But I know better now. Much of it *is* fraud, perhaps the majority of it. But not all of it. Some of it is frighteningly supernatural.

The majority of the psychic surgeons come from the spiritist centers of Brazil and the Philippines. One of the best known is the late Arigo, who attended from three to four hundred people a day—a total of more than two million before his fatal accident.

Psychic surgery is done under unsanitary, even filthy conditions, often with dirty or rusty knives as instruments. No anesthesia is used. And the surgeon pays little attention to his work. Obviously this is because a spirit guide, or spirit doctor, is really performing the surgery. The surgeons are all aware of this and freely admit that they can do nothing without the spirits.

Spirit surgery, along with spirit diagnosis and spirit healing, is coming into our own country. Is this the healing you want? Are you willing to pay the price of a slavery to the occult from which only the Lord Jesus Christ can ever free you?

We hear much about holistic medicine today. And certainly the concept of treating the whole man, of a patient's involvement in his own health care, of preventive medicine—this is all good. Jesus treated the whole man. And for many years before anyone heard of holistic medicine the motto and goal of Loma Linda University's medical school at Loma Linda, California, has been "To Make Man Whole." Seventh-day Adventists have long been promoting this concept.

But with the holistic medicine that is being marketed today there is need of caution. There is need of discernment. We must be able to distinguish between that which is safe and that which is not safe. For some of the trappings of psychic healing have already filtered deeply into holistic medicine. And some things that in themselves are good are now in bad company.

Take biofeedback, for instance. Certainly there is nothing wrong with the machine, with a feedback of body functions. The trouble is that most feedback operators are involved, at least to some extent, with the occult. In fact, Dr. Elmer Green's research indicates that ESP and parapsychological phenomena sometimes occur in all types of biofeedback experimentation, even though they may not be the goals of the training.

How great is the influence of Eastern mysticism and the occult in the holistic health movement? It is overwhelming. It appears that the movement as a whole is dominated, if not controlled, by philosophies completely incompatible with Christianity. Nearly all of the holistic techniques are filled with subtle, and not so subtle, implications that have their origin in the occult. Most of these techniques are designed to produce altered states of consciousness to make their treatments work. And the new energies of the East—dangerous in the extreme!

It is apparent that few of the holistic centers around the country have escaped occult involvement. Their literature reveals this. The courses they teach give it away. It is estimated that probably 80 to 90 percent of the talks given at national holistic health conferences support the occult in one way or another.

You can see, then, that the role of the individual physician to whom we entrust our health care becomes vitally important. Certainly it would be unfair to assume that an individual physician is involved with the occult just because many of his colleagues are. On the other hand, the time has come for extreme caution. It is no longer safe to assume noninvolvement!

You may be saying, "All this is very interesting. Amazing. Even frightening. I've learned a lot."

But friend, until you realize that evil angels are all about us in the unseen world and that they are battling for the control of our minds—yours and mine—you've missed the point. These agents of Satan, if permitted, will distract our minds, disorder and torment our bodies, and destroy our health, our possessions, and our lives. And they will try to use everything that happens to us—everything good and everything bad—to accomplish our total destruction!

On the other hand, Jesus will do *everything He can* to save us. He is stronger than the enemy. And He would sooner send every angel from heaven to our aid than let us pass under the enemy's power against our will!

But we must *ask* for that aid. It will not be forced upon us. You and I, this very moment, with our own permission, are under the control of one power or the other. But the choice is ours!

Wonderful Jesus! What we have learned about the enemy only makes us love Jesus more. For the beauty of His character, in contrast, stands out like a brilliant star against a black night!

Are you letting every enemy attack drive you nearer to the Saviour and deepen your relationship with Him? I hope so. For only in His hands are any of us safe!

Toys of a Fallen Angel

What are those mysterious lights that cavort like cosmic dancers across the night sky? Flitting across the radar screens of the mind—only to disappear. Following us. Eluding us. Dazzling us with their technology. Luring us with their mystery. Baffling us with their uncanny tricks.

What are these strange things that bob up and down like illuminated yo-yos over our hilltops and our highways, our airports, and our cities—defying our restricted air space, skittering away when we point a powerful beam of light their way, and generally frightening us out of our wits?

Are they the toys of some cosmic prankster? Or could it be that *people*—people like you and me—are the toys? Toys of a fallen angel. To be played with a little while—and then thrown away!

It is said that the Rand Corporation, the fabled "think-tank," was once asked to feed UFO data into a computer and fight an imaginary war with the elusive entities. But since we didn't know their origin or their technology or how to attack their bases, the computer advised that we surrender!

Am I going to tell you the UFOs are real? No. Am I going to tell you they aren't? No. It doesn't matter whether they are real or not. Something very real is happening to millions of people. And that *does* matter!

Let me say it once more. Whether or not UFOs exist is not the question. Whether they do or not, something is going on. People are involved with something—whether it is real or unreal. People are letting their lives be completely changed by UFOs. People are making a religion out of UFOs. People are blowing their minds, and losing their minds, over UFOs. People are being injured by UFOs. People are being controlled by UFOs. We need to stop quibbling over whether they are seeing them or not or riding in them or not or telling the truth about them or not—and get on with the business of discovering, if we can, the source of the phenomena. For that we desperately need to know!

It isn't being gullible to recognize that something is going on. The man who is gullible is the man who closes his eyes and his ears and refuses to admit that anything is happening. He is the one being fooled. We have come to a time when it isn't safe to stick your head in the sand—if you care anything about your head!

Something is going on. And nothing is gained by trying to tell experienced pilots that the planet Venus is roaming around between them and the ground. Nothing is accomplished by telling a pilot that the squadron of brilliantly lighted craft that executed incredibly difficult maneuvers at high speed, frighteningly close to his plane, was nothing more than plastic garment bags, with lighted candles inside, released by some teenage boys. Whenever debunking becomes ridiculous, it only acts as a boomerang that quickly destroys the credibility of the debunker!

In our American democracy it seems that we have only two options. We can be a Democrat or be a Republican. And it's like that with UFOs. It is *assumed* that we have but two choices. These strange craft are all nonsense. Or they are extraterrestrial. One or the other.

But I don't believe that we are limited to only two possible explanations. My Bible tells me about a host of intelligent entities, *terrestrially* based, who could easily be back of the whole phenomenon. Listen to what it says: "There was war in heaven. Michael [Christ] and his angels fought against the dragon [Satan], and the dragon and his angels fought back. But he was not strong enough, and they lost their place in heaven. The great dragon was hurled down—that ancient serpent called the devil or Satan, who leads the whole world astray. He was hurled to the earth, and his angels with him." Revelation 12:7-9, NIV.

Verse 3 suggests that a third of all the angels of heaven sided with Satan in this senseless rebellion and were banished to the earth with him. That's a lot of angels—angels now turned demons.

Now I don't want to be dogmatic and say that Satan is the source of the UFO phenomenon. Again, I don't know what UFOs are. They might turn out to be some secret military craft. Some remotely controlled spycraft. Or ball lightning. Or something we haven't thought of yet. But certainly there is a mountain of evidence that points to Satan and his demon helpers as prime suspects.

Here we have a vast number of intelligences once extraterrestrial, created to inhabit heaven, but now operating right here on this earth. And they have the advantage of being able to work invisibly, hidden from our sight. And though banished to our planet, they still have the brilliant minds of angels. They know more about technology than men have ever dreamed. And they have supernatural power, within the limits that God has set.

Jesus warned us that in this end time our planet would be overrun with false prophets and false miracles. He said, "False Christs and false prophets will appear and perform great signs and miracles to deceive even the elect—if that were possible." Matthew 24:24, NIV.

Did you notice? Miracles to deceive. That's why the miracles are worked.

And now to the book of Revelation. "They are spirits of demons performing miraculous signs." Revelation 13:13, 14.

It's speaking of an agent of Satan here. And notice. It doesn't say "miracles which he tried to do" or "miracles which he pretended to do." It says "miracles which he had *power* to do." And those miracles are for the purpose of deceiving those who dwell on the earth.

It's a good thing to get these things straight, don't you think, before we go on.

I think you will agree that the fallen angel, with his army of demon helpers, is well equipped to engineer a phenomenon such as we are discussing. There is no part of it, no feature of it, that is beyond his power.

But I want to say again, It really doesn't matter whether UFOs exist or not, whether they are real or only an illusion. If they do exist, it doesn't matter whether they are made of metal or made of hallucinations. We only mark ourselves as having faulty eyesight if we say nothing is happening. Whatever they are or are not, millions of people are involved with them and are being harmed. They are making a religion of them. And whether Satan is originating the phenomenon or not, he is certainly exploiting the situation to the full!

I know that many attempts have been made to explain the sightings as due to natural causes. For years they have been blamed to the moon, to temperature inversions, light refractions, migrating birds, clouds, mirages, stars, marsh gas, ball lightning—and of course the planet Venus.

But there are patterns in the sightings that soon rule out such explanations and indicate that intelligence of some kind is back of the UFO activity. For instance, in a great many cases the UFOs fly right up to a state line but do not cross it. Why don't they cross it? Certainly meteors cannot read our maps. There are more sightings in isolated areas and in the late evening, suggesting that UFOs, or their occupants, usually prefer to keep their activity secret. There are more sightings on Wednesday and Saturday nights. Can the phenomenon read not only our maps, but also our calendars and our clocks? Some intelligence must be involved. And it doesn't take long to see that the phenomenon is not natural but supernatural.

It is also sensational. And I am aware that some people think we ought not to talk about anything sensational. But that's what Satan and his helpers love. Ever since the encounter in the Garden of Eden it has been their favorite and most successful area of attack. And to refuse to mention anything sensational is to say to Satan, "Look! You just stay within the boundaries of the sensational and we won't bother you."

And that gives the fallen angel and his helpers a free hand!

So let's talk about it. Ever hear of poltergeists? Of course. Noisy ghosts. Did you know that almost always when there is a flap of UFO sightings there is also a flap of poltergeist activity—just before or just after or simultaneously? There's a connection somewhere.

To study the endless sightings of UFOs is not very productive. There are books full of them—and books full of messages that have supposedly come from them. But they are repetitive, and they are boring. It is far better to study the people who see these things— the people who have contact with them. It's the people who are important.

These millions of people from all walks of life, including a great many pilots and policemen—these people are not lying. They may be the victims of lies. But they are describing as truthfully as they can what they saw and what happened and what they have been told!

Strange things happen to people who see these baffling things in the sky—especially to people who have any further contact with them. Their lives soon become a series of bizarre experiences, and anything—or any combination of things—may happen. Their telephones and television sets go berserk. Radios play when they are turned off. Fierce headaches, nausea, and loss of appetite are common.

They are troubled by nightmares. They see frightening apparitions. Poltergeists invade the homes. They have strange visitors and strange phone calls. Mysterious black Cadillacs may appear and disappear suddenly. And the more frightened they become, the more the manifestations escalate!

Soon after the first contact the personality may begin to deteriorate. And the deterioration may become total. Paranoid-schizophrenia and even suicide may result.

This does not for a moment mean that a person who sees a UFO is insane. Not at all. But unless the involvement is broken off, he or she may be *driven* insane by the phenomena.

Did you know that the symptoms experienced by UFO contactees are the same as those of demon possession? Dabbling with UFOs can be extremely dangerous. Even serious investigators take great risks. The conflict between Christ and Satan is not folklore. It is real. Demons are real. And demons are treacherous.

We are dealing here with intelligences who are able to alter the perceptions and produce paranormal states of consciousness. They are able to alter the observer's sense of reality. Powerful imagery is projected upon the mind for the purpose of altering the individual's beliefs and making him a tool of the system of deception.

This may explain the reports of contactees being abducted and taken aboard a UFO. It seems that hypnosis can trigger the account of an abduction experience in almost anybody—that is, anybody uninformed enough and unwise enough to submit the mind to somebody else. This may explain why the abduction stories are so similar—just as the near-death stories of tunnels and grassy slopes and beings of light are similar. We are dealing here not simply with hypnosis, but with thought implant. The subject remembers what the entity in control of his mind wants remembered.

It is probable that these contactees were never taken aboard a flying saucer at all. Remember that these entities are able to manipulate the mind and induce a trance state. If you were to come upon a contactee at the time of his alleged kidnap experience, you might find him standing rigid beside his car or alongside the road. He is not going anywhere at all. What is happening to him is happening only in his mind. It has been implanted there.

Do you begin to see now how dangerous any involvement with UFOs can be? Take the "kidnap" experience, for instance. You may say, "If it never happened, how can it be dangerous?" But nothing is more dangerous than what happens to the mind. The individual *thinks* the abduction happened. And his whole life may be changed by that distortion of reality. And of course that is what the phenomenon is all about. Its goal is to alter belief and behavior and make the contactee a tool of the system.

Well, are the mysterious flying machines really up there in the skies? They are when the demons want them to be!

The UFOs go where they please and when they please. They go merrily on their way, baffling us with their inconsistent behavior, exasperating us with their elusive maneuvers, driving us crazy with their cruel games. And the wise man is he who knows, or at least suspects, who they are—and leaves them alone!

Perhaps we are ready now for the question, Do UFOs really exist at all? Evidently they do not exist in the way a book or a house or a plane exists. But certainly the *phenomenon* exists.

John Keel's book *UFOs Operation Trojan Horse* is probably the most informative and logical book written on the subject. After four years of investigating UFOs—full time, often day and night, without a vacation—he concluded that there are two general types of unidentified flying objects. They might be called the "soft" craft and the "hard" craft.

The "soft" objects are those that are luminous, that

change shape and color at will, that split apart, that appear and disappear before your eyes, baffling explanation. These are the more numerous. And these are evidently the real phenomena. They can only be explained as manifestations of demon power. No other explanation makes sense or fits the facts.

Witnesses, over and over again, have confided in hushed tones to John Keel, "You know, I don't think that thing I saw was mechanical at all. I got the distinct impression that it was *alive*!"

Then, in much smaller number, there are the hard, seemingly solid objects that are seen occasionally. These have been fired upon by bullets—and the bullets have ricocheted off. They sometimes leave prints on the ground when they land. In flight, they frequently drop pieces of metal. John Keel believes that these seemingly hard, metallic UFOs are temporary manipulations of matter and energy, made for a few moments of use—or perhaps a few hours—probably to try to prove that they are real, or just to confuse.

In other words, they are materializations such as are seen in spiritism, where frequently there are materializations of ash trays, bookends, trumpets, etc. And the "ufonauts" dematerialize the craft at will. That's the disappearing act.

The parallels between spiritism and the UFO phenomenon, between demonic activity and UFO activity, are striking. Mediums go into a trance. Contactees go into a trance. Spirits walk through closed doors. UFO entities seem to fly up to their ships and walk or float right through the sides. In both fields human beings and nonhuman objects are transported without visible means. Entities in both fields are able to change their shape at will. Both demons and UFO entities are able to assume the form of human beings—and frequently do.

Devotees of spiritism receive messages supposedly from deceased loved ones. UFO followers receive telephone calls supposedly from space people. Followers of both receive messages that are mentally detected—they hear them in their heads. Both see monsters and apparitions. Hypnotism ranges freely through both fields. Hoaxes are common in both. Demons are accomplished liars. So are UFO entities. Mediums are possessed and controlled and manipulated. So are contactees. Both become not only reporters but mouthpieces.

Do you see *the telltale connection*? Is there any question but that the same powers who operate in the darkened room may also be piloting their cosmic toys?

The man who becomes involved with UFOs in any way is in great danger. But the man who denies the existence of the phenomenon may be in even greater peril—because he is unprepared for the personal encounter that may be in store for him. To deny the reality of the unseen world is to be engulfed by it!

What do these elusive entities want? What is the purpose of all this worldwide propaganda? What is all this leading up to? You will see. And I promise you it's something bigger than you think. What we are witnessing is not overkill. This army of deceivers is not preparing to swat a fly. They have a real extravaganza in mind!

Satan and his demons would love nothing better than to destroy us all—now. But lacking God's permission to wipe out the human race, they will content themselves with making toys of the uninformed and the reckless. Be assured that Satan has no love even for his own. He toys with them a little while, plays mischievous games with them, feeds them nonsense, laughs at their troubles, and then throws them away like paper dolls that have begun to tear!

But friend, not one of us are toys to Jesus. Each one of us, to Him, is of infinite worth. The value of one soul can never be estimated except as we see what it cost Him to set it free!

See Him walking straight on, with His eyes on Calvary—never turning aside, never turning back. Because you were lost. And the only way to save you was to die in your place. See Him in face-to-face combat with the enemy, gaining for you the victory that could never be yours without Him!

See Him in Gethsemane, tempted to the very limit of His endurance. So tempted that He would have died right there in the garden had not an angel come to sustain Him. See Him struggling through His fearful ordeal while His closest friends are sleeping. See Him on the cross, with only the prayer of a thief to cheer Him. He heard no other prayer that day—except His own!

Why didn't He come down from the cross and call a legion of angels to lift Him out of the cruel nightmare of this Golgotha? Why didn't He give up—when it seemed that nobody wanted to be saved anyway? But no. Somewhere a few would accept His sacrifice. And even if only one—He was willing to die if only just one could be rescued from this doomed planet. That's how much He cared—and still cares—for you!

Whoever you are, wherever you are, whatever you have done, however great your guilt may be, He wants to forgive. He wants to be your Saviour. He wants to be your Friend. Your relationship with Him can be as close, as real, as enduring as if you were the only one in the world in need of His love and care!

To Jesus you will never be a toy. To Him you will always be a priceless treasure. He will never tire of you and throw you away. He will be your Friend forever. And you can be His!

The Tiger Behind the Door

It was December 15, 1967.

Watching Lyndon Johnson turn on the lights of the Christmas tree was not exactly an exciting experience. Many of those who watched on television may have reacted with a measure of ho-hum. But not those who had heard the prediction!

Nineteen sixty-seven had been a big year for predictions. One after another the prophecies had come down through mediums and psychics, astrologers and automatic writers, crystal-ball gazers and UFO contactees. Some of the predictions had failed. But others had come true on the nose—enough to make those in-the-know mighty nervous. All agreed that something big—and something disastrous—would happen when Lyndon Johnson pushed the switch. Possibly a nationwide power failure!

And so, glued to their television screens, they watched breathlessly. When the lights of the Christmas tree went on, would the lights of the nation go out?

The president pushed the switch. The lights of the tree went on. And nothing happened. But thirty seconds later an announcer's voice came over the noise of the crowd. "We interrupt this program for a special bulletin. A bridge with rush-hour traffic has just collapsed at Gallipolis, Ohio. Further details as soon as they are available."

The bridge at Gallipolis, Ohio. That could only be the 700-foot Silver Bridge that connected Gallipolis with Point Pleasant, West Virginia.

And Point Pleasant, for exactly thirteen months, had been the target of some very strange goings-on. More than a hundred people had been frightened by a huge monster with red glowing eyes. It was shaped like a man, maybe seven feet tall, with huge folded wings. They called him Mothman. You can read about this in John Keel's book, *The Mothman Prophecies*.

But that was not all. People had been seeing UFOs all summer. There were dozens of witnesses.

There were the strange men in black. Men who seemed unacquainted with the area, or even with this planet. Men whose shoe soles were perfectly clean after walking through mud. Men whose features were strangely alike. Men who wore thin clothing in the dead of winter. Men who talked like phonograph records speeded up.

There was Indrid Cold—he said that was his name. He said he was from the planet Lanulos. He drove a black Volkswagen—and sometimes a spaceship—and was generous with his strange and irrelevant information.

There were the black Cadillacs that kept disappearing when they were chased. With license numbers that no computer could trace. There were the strange phone calls, the phantom photographers, the TV sets that went berserk. For some Point Pleasant residents, everything seemed to be going berserk.

But neither Mothman nor Indrid Cold—nor any of the UFO entities—ever said a word about the coming disaster.

And then it happened!

Some who had seen Mothman—or been participants in other bizarre experiences during the year—went down with the bridge. Others would be claimed by death within a short time. Some would divorce. Some would suffer breakdowns and undergo long periods of hospitalization. A few would commit suicide.

Twelve UFOs were over Point Pleasant at the time the bridge went down. And some strange-looking men, wearing thin shoes in the cold, had been seen climbing on the bridge two days earlier. Was there any connection?

But if the strange entities knew about the coming disaster, or even participated in it, why hadn't they warned Point Pleasant?

We could ask the same question about Jonestown. With all the predictions from the various psychics, how is it that we were not warned that the horrifying suicide/massacre would take place?

I believe the answer to that question would not be difficult when we understand a little more about these psychic predictions.

I wonder if you are aware that six different psychics predicted the capture of Patty Hearst with uncanny accuracy. And the deaths of the Kennedy brothers and Martin Luther King were predicted again and again in different parts of the world.

Significantly, predictions like these, whoever the prophet and wherever the forecast is made, seem to be coming from a common source. Evidently there is a prediction syndicate operating somewhere!

The very same predictions are often fed through a number of different psychic channels. They are released through mediums and mystics, psychics and astrologers, automatic writers and crystal-ball gazers, Ouija boards and UFO contactees. Clearly they are all tuned in to the same source. UFO entities and spirit entities are part of the same gigantic system. The link is undeniable. In fact, the communication that takes place between a medium and the spirit world, the communication that takes place in the near-death experiences, the communication between UFO contactees and UFO entities, the communication between psychic healers and their spirit-doctors—in all these the communicators on the other side, in the unseen world, are the same evil spirits, the same fallen angels, the same demons. They are simply adapting what they say to their particular audience.

Psychic predictions are often phrased identically, regardless of the channels through which they are released. This is true throughout the country—and throughout the world. The messages are often even *phrased* in the same way—no matter what language is used!

We can only conclude that psychic predictions have a common source. And if that source is ultimately Satan himself, it is not especially hard to understand why disasters like the Silver Bridge—and Jonestown—were not predicted. For Satan genuinely loves disasters. And the more lives that are snuffed out, the more pleased he is.

Predictions in the year 1967 included a big power failure, New York sliding into the sea, the assassination of Pope Paul, plane crashes, a bigger power failure nationwide in scope, a disaster on the Ohio River, the

Prime Minister of Australia disappearing, and explosions in Moscow.

All these happened on the nose, except the nationwide power failure, the assassination of Pope Paul, and Manhatten sliding into the sea. No location on the Ohio River had been pinpointed, so it was only a very general prediction. And the date on which the disaster happened had been linked by the entities—probably intentionally—with a nationwide power failure.

Do you see a pattern here? Some predictions come true. Some don't. In general, the minor ones are the most often accurate. The really major ones—like Manhatten slipping into the sea—are less likely to be accurate. Why is this?

Do these psychic entities know the future? Or don't they? Why isn't this giant prediction syndicate right all the time—if it knows the future?

The answer is that the entities do *not* know the future. Only God knows the future. And when He reveals it through His prophets, they are right all the time—not just some of the time.

The entities who run the prophecy syndicate do not know the future. But they know their own plans. They certainly do have an agenda for the future which they intend to follow if they can!

Keep in mind that God does restrict them to some extent and allows them to go only so far. But within the limits set by God they are able to engineer many a disaster. It's a simple matter to arrange the collapsing of an aging bridge. They can crash planes—if God doesn't prevent them. They are often right about marriages and divorces, because they are able to listen in on the most private of conversations. They are present in the carefully locked rooms where crimes are planned. And minds under the control of demons can often be influenced to carry out assassinations.

But pushing Manhattan or California into the sea is too much for the fallen angel and his helpers. Nothing of such major consequence will happen unless and until God permits it!

Do you see now why the predictions of the psychics are usually concerned with marriages, divorces, plane crashes, assassinations, etc? The fallen angel predicts what he thinks he may have a good chance of accomplishing. But the stately march of prophecy that you find in the Bible—affecting nations and the world, and penetrating the future with an accuracy that never fails—is simply beyond these impostors!

But wait. Sometimes they do predict big things like the end of the world, don't they? Yes, they do.

For instance, take the case of Dr. Charles A. Laughead. He was a physician on the staff of Michigan State University when he started communicating with entities who claimed to be from outer space in 1954. A number of minor prophecies were passed along to him, and they came true on the nose. Then came the big one. The world was going to be split in two, and the Atlantic Coast would sink into the sea. France, England, and Russia would have the same fate. But a few select people would be rescued by spaceships.

Dr. Laughead and his friends were so impressed by the accuracy of the previous predictions that they took this one very seriously. He made sober declarations to the press. Then on December 21 they gathered in a garden to wait for rescue. They had been told not to wear any metal. So they discarded belt buckles and clasps, pens and lighters—even shoes with metal eyelets.

Then they waited!

It has happened again and again. Men and women become involved. They are convinced by the accuracy of a few predictions. The entities smother them with promises—and then lead them down the road to ruin. Jobs are gone, careers sacrificed, families broken, health destroyed. They hide themselves away and stare at the walls. And the embarrassment and shame and frustration all too often lead to suicide or madness or death.

That's the way the game is played. The entities engineer the fulfillment of a few minor predictions. And then just when men and women are convinced that the entities know everything about the future, they toss in a big one—and leave their trusting followers waiting on some hilltop for spaceships that never come. It's a heartless game. It has been called "the tiger behind the door of prophecy."

And that isn't all. People looking on are harmed too. They see these major predictions fail again and again. And they decide to have nothing to do with prophecy— even Bible prophecy. And that is a dangerous mistake!

Why are people taken in by these psychic hoaxes? One reason is that they do not know what the Bible teaches, though they could have known. Or they *do know* what it teaches and have rejected it. The apostle tells us that many people will be fatally deceived *because* they rejected truth. Listen: "They perish because they refused to love the truth and so be saved. For this reason God sends them a powerful delusion so that they will believe the lie." 2 Thessalonians 2:10, 11, NIV.

Now this doesn't mean that God *originates* the delusion. But when men and women definitely and finally refuse truth, God *permits* them to be overcome by Satan's powerful delusions.

A second reason people are taken in is that they believe everything supernatural is from God. Notice this: "The coming of the lawless one will be in accordance with the work of Satan displayed in all kinds of counterfeit miracles, signs and wonders." 2 Thessalonians 2:9.

The work of Satan in these last days will include all kinds of counterfeit miracles. This is what we can expect. And if we insist on thinking that all these miracles come from God, we haven't a chance!

The third reason people are taken in is that they are reckless concerning their own safety. What do I mean? Simply this: There are people who make their homes a fortress with bolts and locks. They want to protect themselves against the Hillside Strangler and the Trailside Killer and the South Hill Rapist and all the rest. But they will let demons into their homes—demons masquerading as deceased loved ones or spirit guides or spirit doctors or whatever—and let them take control of their lives without ever questioning their identity or their truthfulness. That, I say, is recklessness!

Then the fourth reason people are taken in is that they find the things taught by demons more attractive than truth. The apostle Paul wrote to Timothy, "The Spirit clearly says that in later times some will abandon the faith and follow deceiving spirits and things taught by demons." 1 Timothy 4:1, NIV.

They find truth uninteresting. And truth asks for a commitment. In contrast, they find it exciting to think they are communicating with deceased loved ones or space people. And the teachings of demons make no demands of them—except the surrender of their minds and a lifetime of bondage. But they find that out too late!

Just what do demons teach? What are the doctrines of devils? Spiritism teaches

1. that it is possible to communicate with the dead;
2. that man will never die, that he is immortal and cannot die;
3. that man can become like God, or even become God, that there is divinity within each of us;
4. that there is no future judgment;
5. that at death everybody goes to the same good place, wherever that may be, regardless of how he or she has lived;
6. that in future lives there will be opportunity to correct the wrongs done in this one.

There they are—the telltale marks of the fallen angel's teaching. Easy to recognize. If you're alert.

Well, what does the fallen angel have in mind? What is all his propaganda leading up to? I think you will see.

In May, 1967, a man named Knud Weiking, in Denmark, began receiving a series of telepathic messages which included several prophecies that came true. Then he was told to build a lead-lined bomb shelter and prepare for a holocaust on December 24. He did. He and his friends managed to complete the $30,000 shelter in about three weeks. On December 24 they locked themselves in their bomb shelter and waited.

The Danish cult was not alone, however, in being apprehensive about December 24. Mediums and sensitives and UFO contactees throughout the world were getting identical messages. Something unprecedented was going to happen on that date. At midnight a great light would appear in the sky—and that would be it!

After December 24 had passed, the American press ridiculed the Danish cult for being taken in. But Knud Weiking had an explanation. He said he had received this message: "I told you two thousand years ago that a time would be given and even so I would not come. If you had read your Bible a little more carefully, you would have borne in mind the story of the bridegroom who did not come at the time he was expected. Be watchful so that you are not found without oil in your lamps. I have told you I will come with suddenness, and I shall be coming soon."

Is that what the fallen angel is up to? Does he have in mind pulling off a second coming of his own—ahead of the real one—complete with a phony Christ and phony angels? Are they doing some practice runs to see how their network is operating? Is that what the UFO entities are rehearsing for—the big one to come?

It could be!

Remember Dr. Laughead and his followers—waiting for the end of the world?

And remember those twenty people who disappeared from an Oregon town—because they were promised a trip by UFO to a better world?

There have been others. And there most certainly will be more!

But listen! What we are witnessing, and what is happening behind the scenes, involves far more than UFOs. It's the entities back of the UFOs. It's all of spiritism. It's the whole occult world!

It's possible that UFOs may play no part at all in the counterfeiting of Christ and His second coming. I don't know. But I do know Christ will be impersonated. And it would surprise me if UFOs were not involved in some way. It's difficult to see why the enemy would engineer all this conditioning of millions of people if he didn't intend to move in and turn the popular interest in extraterrestrials to his own ends.

The fallen angel has been in this impersonation game for thousands of years. He has impersonated dead people and living people and space people. Don't you think he'll go for the big one? Don't you think he'll impersonate Jesus too? Worship is what he is after. That's the name of the treacherous game he's playing!

Ellen White describes in *The Great Controversy*, page 624, the impersonation of Christ as if she were an eyewitness. Listen:

"As the crowning act in the great drama of deception, Satan himself will personate Christ. The church has long professed to look to the Saviour's advent as the consummation of her hopes. Now the great deceiver will make it appear that Christ has come. In different parts of the earth, Satan will manifest himself among men as a majestic being of dazzling brightness, resembling the description of the Son of God given by John in the Revelation. . . . The glory that surrounds him is unsurpassed by anything that mortal eyes have yet beheld. The shout of triumph rings out upon the air: 'Christ has come! Christ has come!' The people prostrate themselves in adoration before him, while he lifts up his hands and pronounces a blessing upon them, as Christ himself blessed His disciples when He was upon the earth. His voice is soft and subdued, yet full of melody. In gentle, compassionate tones he presents some of the same gracious, heavenly truths which the Saviour uttered; he heals the diseases of the people, and then, in his assumed character of Christ, he claims to have changed the [law of God]. . . . This is the strong, almost overmastering delusion."

Do you see what is coming? Do you see where the world is being led? Do you see the monstrous hoax for which millions are being subtly conditioned?

The rebel chief may let some of his helpers play savior now—in the rehearsals. But when his extravaganza goes on for real, you can be sure he won't leave the starring role to others. He'll play it himself. It's he who wants the worship. And he'll get it. Almost the whole world will bow down to a masquerading Satan—believing him to be Christ!

What a tragedy that millions upon millions will have neglected the Book that would have saved them, will have tampered with the enemy's tricks, will have become involved with his phony phenomena, will have voluntarily submitted their minds and bodies to his control—until it all ends at the feet of a masquerading imposter! And there will be no way back!

Remember Francis Gary Powers—shot down over Russia in the U-2 incident? He survived that. Years later he was piloting a news helicopter for NBC television in Los Angeles. It was a bad year for fires. He and his cameraman were covering the big Santa Barbara fire. Flying in and out of the canyons, they were excited about the fantastic pictures they had for the five-o'clock news. So excited that the condition of their own fuel tank was forgotten. They crashed in a plowed field two miles from the airport—and both men were dead!

Friend, never was it more important to be alert and aware of what the fallen angel is doing. To be uninformed is to be in peril. But even with the right information wouldn't it be a tragedy if we were to become so absorbed in watching the enemy's strange, hypnotic fires that we forget the state of our own relationship with the Lord Jesus—the Source of all power? We are so near the airport, so near our final landing. It would be stupid to lose out now. Our only safety is in being *aware* of the fallen angel—but *in love* with Jesus!

The Spectacular Finish

God must love the spectacular. He splashes His paints across the evening sky and creates the beauty we frame. He makes a sea out of glass—to reflect the bold and breathless colors of His throne. He builds His streets out of gold instead of concrete. He calls upon the wind, with a touch of lightning and the crashing cymbals of His thunder—to be His overture. He has more galaxies than any computer can count. And I wonder if He leaves one empty just for fireworks—for His pleasure and ours.

But the greatest spectaculars of all He tucks into places like very dark days—and human hearts. And then He turns back to planning the spectacular finish of what we call time. Because He'll be needing it before long!

It was June 14, 1975.

Murray and Roslyn Hughes, eight years old and six, were in the back seats of the plane—their shoes off and their seatbelts tight—when it crashed in a remote section of the Australian Outback. They were not hurt. But their father slumped unconscious in the pilot seat, and their mother was pinned in the cockpit.

Murray couldn't forget the desperation in his mother's voice as she cried, "Take Rossie and go get help! Don't stop for anything!"

The children couldn't find their shoes, so they started out without them. And for twelve hours they stumbled barefoot down the snake-infested mountainside, thinking only of their broken and bleeding parents up there in the fog-enshrouded forest.

Again and again they prayed, "Please, God, make us brave!"

A rancher spotted them in a pasture seven miles from the wreckage. He said, "They were just babies. I couldn't believe it when I saw them out there." They were shivering from the cold, their clothes in tatters. They were badly scratched up, and their feet were bleeding.

"The little girl was very brave," said the rancher, "clutching a small purse with a brush and comb inside. The boy came up and told me to get help for his mother and father. He was the bravest boy I'd ever come across. His feet were cut up real bad, but he didn't want to rest. He had just one thought in mind—to get help for his parents."

The organizer of the rescue party said, "You may think twelve hours isn't long. But this is the toughest country there is. It's dense forest, and the bush is alive with deadly snakes and poisonous spiders. I don't think those two kids could have survived very much longer out there."

Roslyn told about their ordeal. She said, "Mommy told us to be brave and go for help. It was very misty and we couldn't see where we were going. The trees had big roots sticking out of the ground and I kept tripping over them.

"The ground was very rough," she said. "Mommy told us to take our shoes off in the plane so that we would be more comfortable, and when the crash happened we couldn't find them. It hurt when we walked on the ground. There were rough stones and I kept stubbing my toes."

And she went on, "We were very scared. We kept hearing rustling noises all around us. Once, there was a very loud rustling in the bushes right next to us. I screamed. Murray was very brave. He put his arm around me, and said, 'Don't worry. I won't let anything hurt you.' "

Murray said, "I was very scared, but I didn't want Rossie to know. I just kept thinking about Mommy and Daddy and how we had to get help. I have never walked so far. The worst part was having no shoes. . . . Every now and then Rossie would stop and cry. Sometimes I would let her lie down for a while."

The rescue party was too late. And Murray wept, "I only wish we could tell Mommy and Daddy we tried our best!"

How like what Jesus did! People He had made, on a planet He had made, were in trouble. Without help they couldn't survive. And He said, "I'll go, Father." And the Father said, "Go, Son. And don't stop for anything!"

He left His crown behind. It would have been easier with His crown—so much easier. But He didn't stop for anything. All He could think of was finding help— finding a way to save you and me. And again and again He prayed, "Father, make Me brave!"

And so He came to Bethlehem!

When He was twelve years old He visited the magnificent temple. For the first time He saw the priests offering innocent lambs on the altar. He was fascinated by what He saw. There was something mysterious about it—something that seemed to be tied to His own life. And then suddenly He understood. Now it was clear to Him. He Himself was to be the Lamb. He Himself was to be the innocent Sacrifice for men's sins. He Himself was the Way to save a lost race. That's why He had come!

And so He kept straight on to Calvary. All He could think of was men and women who were lost. He had to go on. He was the Lamb!

We have a choice as to how the story ends. It can end with you and me slumped in the cockpit of a wrecked planet. Or it can end in the most spectacular rescue of all time—if we are willing!

But when it's all over, when the last man has made his choice, and when millions have chosen to go down with this planet, I seem to hear the Saviour saying, "Father, I just wish I could tell them I tried My best!"

Is it possible that we are confused about what is really spectacular? The cross of Calvary is the most spectacular event of all time. It's God's incredible exhibit before the court of the universe. It's His unanswerable answer to the charges of those—Satan first among them—who said He didn't care!

If you want the spectacular, you won't have to wait long. God will soon oblige. God is letting Satan do his miracles first. Then God will do His. And Satan's, in comparison, will look like silly tricks!

No words can describe the day when God takes over. Our boasted megatons will seem like popping corn when God takes the affairs of this earth in hand. And Satan can only stand by and watch—helpless, amazed, and terrified!

The fallen angel with his toys can stop a few motors. But God can stop history! Satan can set compasses spinning. But God can defy gravity and lift His people into the sky—and take them home! Satan's UFOs can scorch a little piece of earth. But God can set the mountains smoking with His presence! Satan can bring fire from heaven to deceive men. But God, with fire, can destroy the earth and make it new again! Satan can trace a mysterious image on a piece of film. But God can trace His own image on human hearts! Satan can cause the personality to deteriorate. But God can make men new. And transformed lives are the greatest miracle of all!

The life of the trusting Christian is one constant spectacular. It is a succession of miracles. And God's clock is precisely accurate. He is never late. No emergency takes Him by surprise!

We don't have to worry about God's timing. Over and over it has been demonstrated that His providence can tread safely over circumstances so precarious that the slightest wind could blow a traveler off course, where just a word left unsaid, a seemingly trivial matter neglected, could block the divine plan. How do I know? Because I've seen it—personally—times without number!

Wouldn't you like to have been watching the day God stepped out into space and called our world into existence? He just spoke the word. And there it was! See Psalm 33:6, 9. And then He hung it out into space—on nothing! See Job 26:7.

I like the colorful way Dr. Shadrack Meshack Lockridge pictures it. Listen:

"Standing on nothing, He reached out where there was nowhere to reach and caught something when there was nothing to catch, and hung something on nothing, and told it to stay there. . . . Standing on nothing He took the hammer of His own will, and He struck the anvil of His omnipotence and sparks flew therefrom and He caught them on the tips of His fingers and flung them out into space and bedecked the heavens with stars!"

However God did it, it was a spectacular for sure!

And then there was the Flood of Noah's day. Nothing we've ever experienced can qualify us to understand what happened. Water coming from the clouds in mighty cataracts. Water gushing forth from the earth. Lightning tearing across the sky. Mountains rising and falling. Wind and fire and volcanoes. Tidal waves. The earth torn and twisted and convulsed. A negative spectacular that left only eight people alive!

I was about to say that you and I may have grandstand seats for the spectacular windup of history—the return of Jesus to this earth. But that is hardly correct. There won't be any grandstand seats. There won't be any spectators. Because every man, woman, and child will be personally involved, and the nature of that involvement is up to the individual!

With words borrowed from an inspired pen, let me picture that day:

"It is at midnight that God manifests His power for the deliverance of His people. The sun appears, shining in its strength. Signs and wonders follow in quick succession. The wicked look with terror and amazement upon the scene, while the righteous behold with solemn joy the tokens of their deliverance. Everything in nature seems turned out of its course. The streams cease to flow. Dark, heavy clouds come up and clash against each other. In the midst of the angry heavens is one clear space of indescribable glory, whence comes the voice of God like the sound of many waters, saying 'It is done.'

"That voice shakes the heavens and the earth. There is a mighty earthquake. . . . The firmament appears to open and shut. The glory from the throne of God seems flashing through. The mountains shake like a reed in the wind, and ragged rocks are scattered on every side. There is a roar as of a coming tempest. The sea is lashed into fury. There is heard the shriek of the hurricane like the voice of demons upon a mission of destruction. The whole earth heaves and swells like the waves of the sea. Its surface is breaking up. Its very foundations seem to be giving way. Mountain chains are sinking. Inhabited islands disappear. The seaports that have become like Sodom for wickedness are swallowed up by the angry waters. . . . Great hailstones, every one 'about the weight of a talent [about a hundred pounds]' are doing their work of destruction. . . . The proudest cities of the earth are laid low. . . .

"Fierce lightnings leap from the heavens, enveloping the earth in a sheet of flame. Above the terrific roar of thunder, voices, mysterious and awful, declare the doom of the wicked. . . . Those who a little before were so reckless, so boastful and defiant . . . are now overwhelmed with consternation and shuddering in fear. Their wails are heard above the sound of the elements. Demons acknowledge the deity of Christ and tremble before His power, while men are supplicating for mercy and groveling in abject terror. . . .

"Through a rift in the clouds there beams a star whose brilliancy is increased fourfold in contrast with the darkness. It speaks hope and joy to the faithful, but severity and wrath to the transgressors of God's law. . . .

"Soon there appears in the east a small black cloud, about half the size of a man's hand. It is the cloud which surrounds the Saviour and which seems in the distance to be shrouded in darkness. The people of God know this to be the sign of the Son of man. In solemn silence they gaze upon it as it draws nearer the earth, becoming lighter and more glorious, until it is a great white cloud, its base a glory like consuming fire, and above it the rainbow of the covenant. Jesus rides forth as a mighty conqueror. . . . With anthems of celestial melody the holy angels, a vast, unnumbered throng, attend Him on His way. . . . No human pen can portray the scene; no mortal mind is adequate to conceive its splendor."—*The Great Controversy,* pp. 636-641.

A scene spectacular beyond words!

But listen. The cross of Calvary is even more spectacular than the return of Jesus to this earth. His return to this planet can be understood. Calvary never can. Not fully. Not by men. Not by angels. Not by the residents of unfallen worlds!

Calvary! The most tragic day of all history. Men nailing their Creator to a cross! But it was also a day for great rejoicing. Men didn't know what was happening that day. But angels did. When they heard the Son of God cry out from the cross, "It is finished!" they knew its significance for all the universe. Jesus had reached the finish line. He had fallen dead across it. But He had reached it. Without sinning once. Not one temptation, not one test of His faith or His patience, not one trick of the enemy, had left the slightest taint upon Him. He was a perfect Saviour!

But the men He had come to save—didn't want to be saved!

Imagine—if you can—what a scandalous tragedy it would have been if Murray and Roslyn had stumbled down that treacherous mountainside as they did, and the rescue party had reached their parents in time— only to be told that they didn't want to be rescued. After all it had cost to make rescue possible!

But that's what some of us are doing to our Lord!

He went through infinitely more than those two devoted children. He walked through serpent-infested country for thirty-three years—and went home to His Father with His hands and His feet scarred for eternity by the daring rescue attempt. Will we tell Him we don't want to be rescued after all?

Thirty-three years! And He never turned back. Sometimes He was so weary, so faint and exhausted, so crushed by it all, that the angels let Him rest a few moments in their arms. But He kept thinking of you and me—and He had to go on. He was the Lamb of God. And He had an appointment with a rough and rugged cross outside Jerusalem. A cross that should have been yours. And mine!

Friend, it's perfectly safe to let Jesus capture your heart!